First published by Parragon in 2009

Parragon
Queen Street House
4 Queen Street
Bath BA1 1HE, UK

www.chuggington.com

© Ludorum plc 2009

ISBN 978-1-4075-6041-0

Printed in China

CLUNKY WILSON

Based on the episode "Clunky Wilson,"
written by Sarah Ball and Kate Fawkes.

Bath · New York · Singapore · Hong Kong · Cologne · Delhi · Melbourne

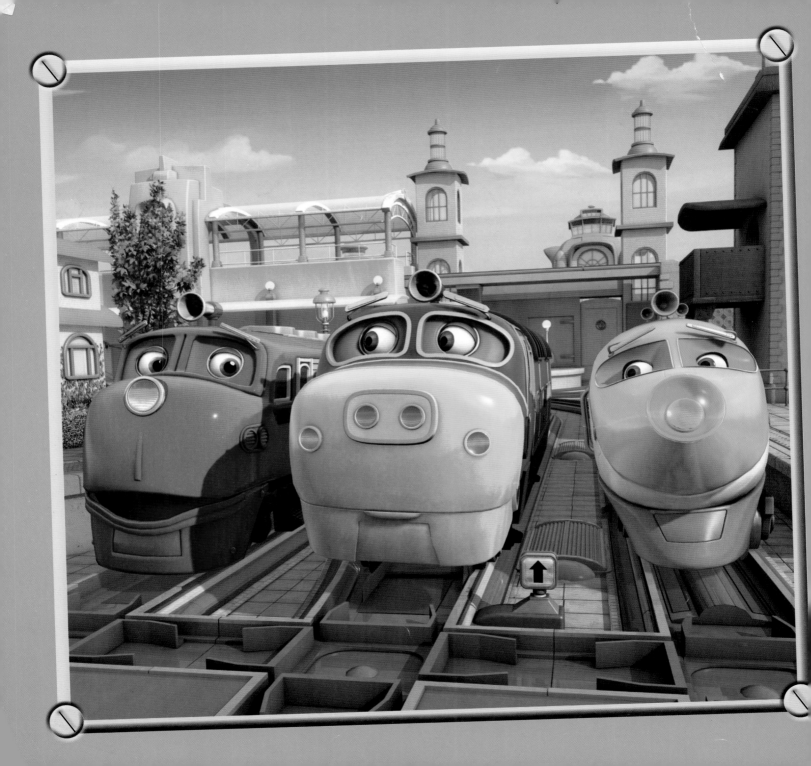

One day, Chuggington trainees Wilson, Koko and Brewster, were ready to have a race.

Suddenly, they heard some horrible sounds coming from the repair shed.

CLUNK! CLANK! CLANG!

"What's that noise?" Wilson asked, his voice a bit wobbly.

Koko dared him to go and look but Wilson wouldn't.

TOOT! TOOT!

"Chugger approaching," called Emery, a cheeky white train. "Hey, whatcha all doing?"

"Wilson's too scared to find out what the sounds from the repair shed are," teased Koko.

"Puffer Pete was inside there for a whole week once," Emery said. "They took all his wheels off!"

Wilson gasped. He never wanted to go to the repair shed.

READING'S FUN!

HONK! HONK!

"Let's race," said Koko. "Last one to the bumpers has square wheels!"

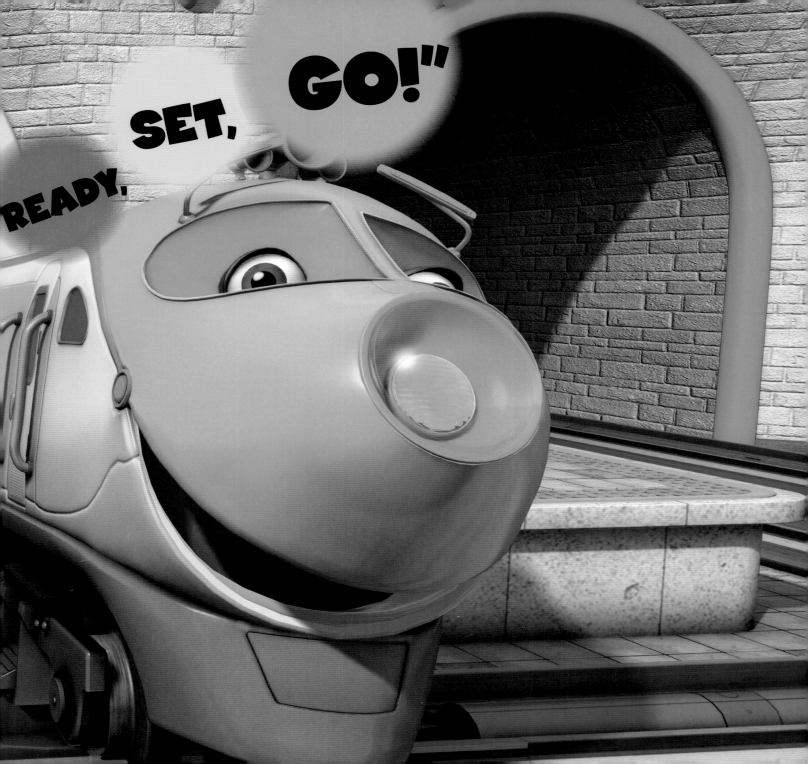

Speedy Koko zoomed off.
But Wilson was determined
to beat her for once.
"I can do it!" he cried.

Meanwhile, poor Brewster began to puff – he just couldn't keep up with the others!

CHUGGA, CHUGGA! CHOO, CHOO!

Koko slowed down as she neared the bumpers at the end of the track. But Wilson didn't see them. He tried to stop but it was too late!

SCREEEEECH..... CRASH!

Wilson crashed into the bumpers. As he reversed, his wheels made a terrible noise. Something was wrong...

Just then, Vee made an announcement.

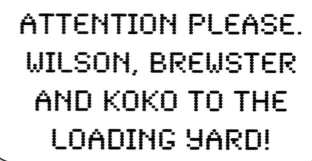

ATTENTION PLEASE.
WILSON, BREWSTER
AND KOKO TO THE
LOADING YARD!

"Wahay!" said Wilson, excitedly.
"It's training time!"
But as Wilson followed Koko and
Brewster to the depot, his wheels
made a scraping sound.

SCRAPE!
SCRAPE!

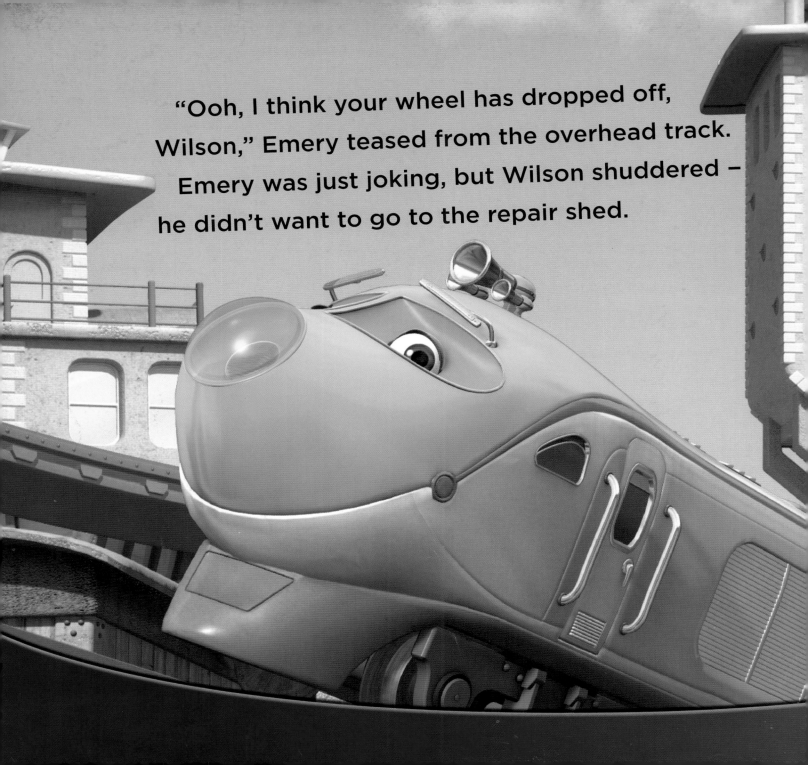

"Ooh, I think your wheel has dropped off, Wilson," Emery teased from the overhead track. Emery was just joking, but Wilson shuddered – he didn't want to go to the repair shed.

In the loading yard, Wilson buckled up to a boxcar. His wheels were still making funny noises.

CLUNKETY, CLUNK!

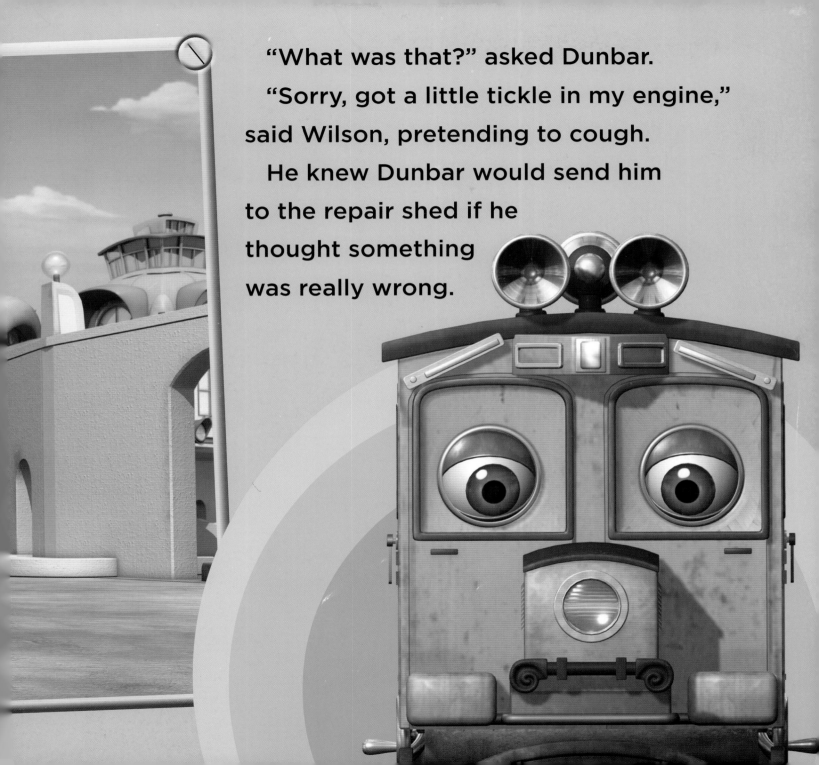

"What was that?" asked Dunbar.

"Sorry, got a little tickle in my engine," said Wilson, pretending to cough.

He knew Dunbar would send him to the repair shed if he thought something was really wrong.

Vee sent the three trainee chuggers to take some things from the farm to the fair.

Koko loaded her boxcar with eggs, Brewster took some vegetables and Wilson got the cream.

Felix the farmer asked Wilson if he could ride with him to the fair too. He was hoping his cream would win a prize. But the journey was so bumpy...

RATTLE!
RATTLE!

...poor Felix spilled his carton of juice!

It was no good. Wilson couldn't ignore his problem any longer. He would have to go to the repair shed!

The red chugger shakily followed his friends back to the depot.

CLUNKETY, CLANK!

In the repair shed, Morgan the mechanic put Wilson on the rotator, so he could look underneath him.

"You're really brave," Morgan told Wilson. "Most chuggers are nervous the first time they have to get fixed." That made Wilson feel better. And soon, Morgan had mended Wilson's broken suspension spring. Wilson was as good as new!

Later that day, Vee called Wilson back to the fair to collect Felix.

Felix told Wilson that the bumpy ride shook the cream up so much that it was really thick. Wilson felt terrible.

"Instead, the judges thought it was the most delicious butter they had ever tasted," said Felix.

Wilson beamed with pride as Felix placed his first prize rosette on him.

"But next time there's something wrong with me, I'm going straight to the repair shed!"

Visit **VIRTUAL CHUGGINGTON**

www.chuggington.com

Now you can ride the rails with Wilson, Koko and Brewster!

Honk your horns! Here in Chuggington we need more little engines to join us and keep things ship-shape. That means you, trainee!

- ○ Paint your own engine
- ○ Meet the chuggers
- ○ Finish training tasks
- ○ Play games
- ○ Earn badges

Attention grown-ups!

Virtual Chuggington is a digital world where children can experience life from the same perspective as the engines. Think of it as a digital train set, one with an open-ended play pattern and storytelling capability that will awaken your child's sense of wonder!

Join us here, won't you? We can't wait to learn, work and play together!

www.chuggington.com